## Exploring the Galaxy

# Stars

by Thomas K. Adamson

**Consulting Editor:** Gail Saunders-Smith, PhD

**Consultant:** Roger D. Launius, PhD
Chair, Division of Space History
National Air and Space Museum
Smithsonian Institution, Washington, D.C.

Capstone press
Mankato, Minnesota

Pebble Plus is published by Capstone Press,
151 Good Counsel Drive, P.O. Box 669, Mankato, Minnesota 56002.
www.capstonepub.com

*Library of Congress Cataloging-in-Publication Data*
Adamson, Thomas K., 1970–
    Stars / by Thomas K. Adamson.
    p. cm.—(Pebble plus. Exploring the galaxy)
    Includes bibliographical references and index.
    ISBN 978-0-7368-6746-7 (hardcover)
    ISBN 978-1-4296-6291-8 (softcover)
    1. Stars—Juvenile literature. I. Title. II. Series.
QB801.7.A28 2007
523.8—dc22                                                          2006023559

Summary: Simple text and photographs describe stars.

**Editorial Credits**
Katy Kudela, editor; Kia Adams, set designer; Mary Bode, book designer; Jo Miller, photo researcher/photo editor

**Photo Credits**
Comstock Images, 1, 12–13
Corbis/Matthias Kulka, 4–5
Getty Images Inc./Iconica/Jeff Spielman, 9
Photodisc, cover
Photo Researchers, Inc./Celestial Image Co., 15; David Nunuk, 20–21; European Southern Observatory, 17; Gerard Lodriguss, 19;
    Jerry Schad, 10–11; John Chumack, 7

## Note to Parents and Teachers

The Exploring the Galaxy set supports national science standards related to earth science. This book describes and illustrates stars. The photographs support early readers in understanding the text. The repetition of words and phrases helps early readers learn new words. This book also introduces early readers to subject-specific vocabulary words, which are defined in the Glossary section. Early readers may need assistance to read some words and to use the Table of Contents, Glossary, Read More, Internet Sites, and Index sections of the book.

Printed in China
5888/5889/5890    082010

# Table of Contents

# Stars

Stars appear in the sky
on a clear night.
They look like
tiny points of light.

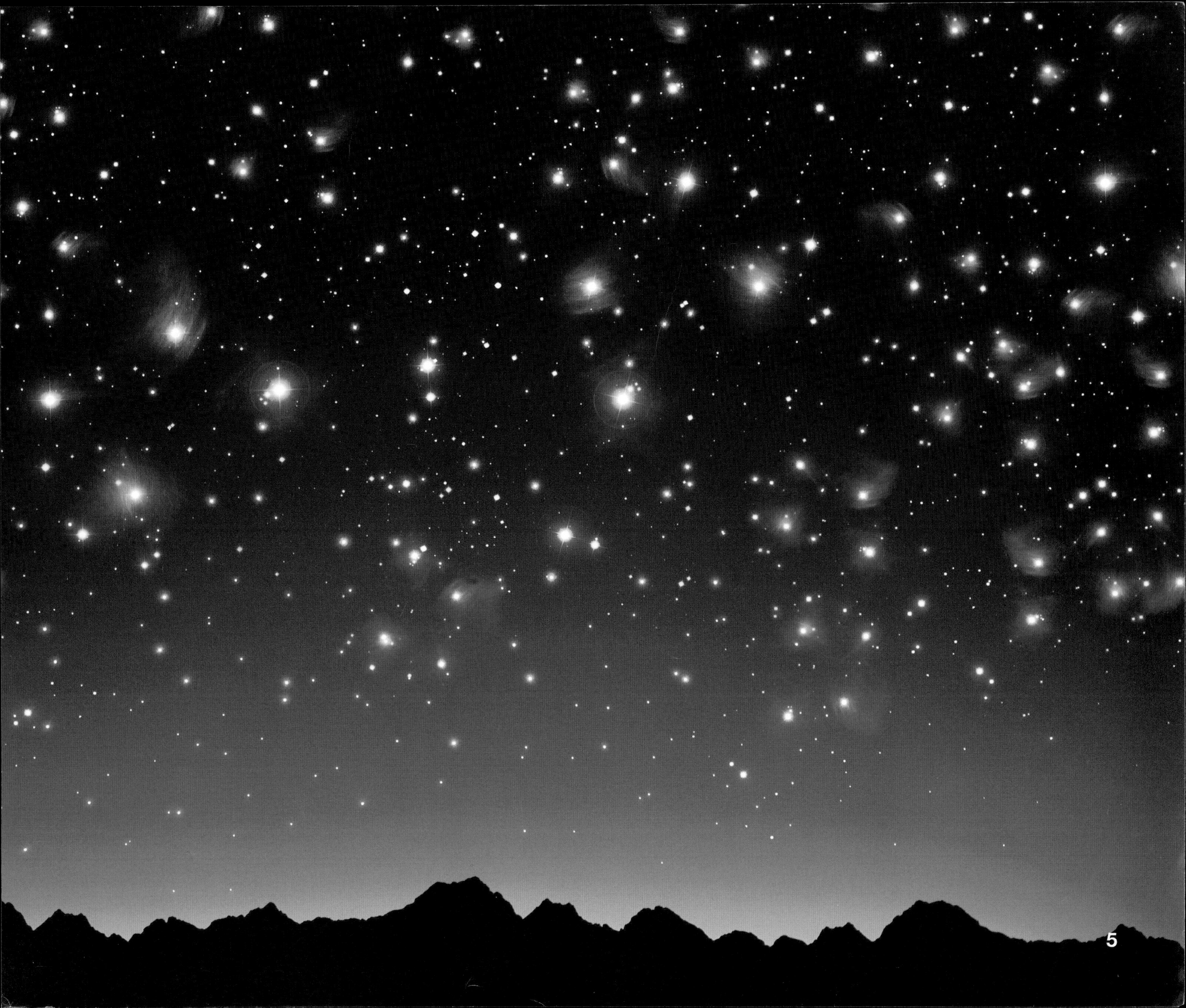

Stars are giant balls
of hot gases.
The gases give off
light and heat.

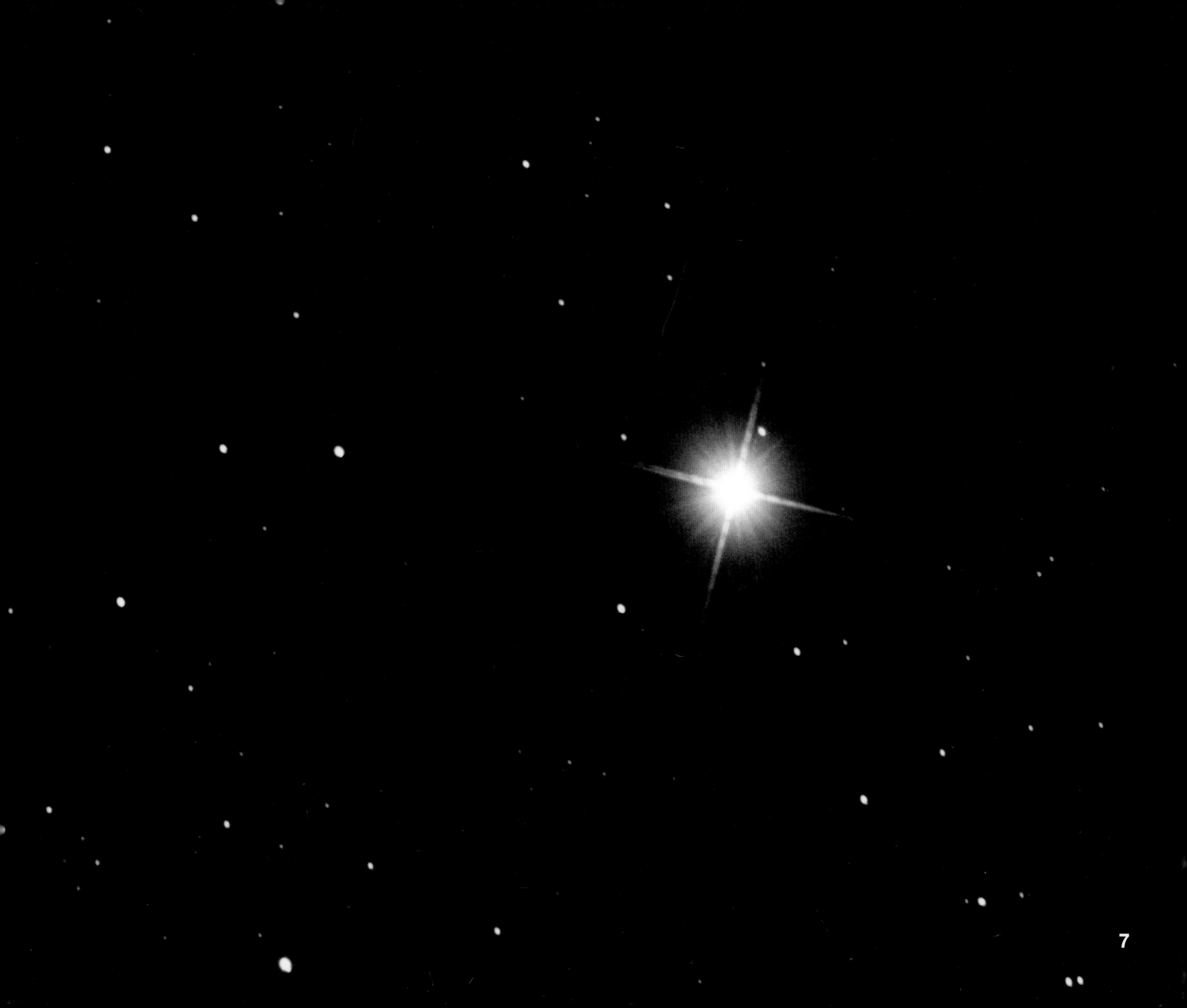

# Stars and Earth

The Sun is the easiest star
to find in the sky.
It is the closest star
to Earth.

Other stars show up at night.

These stars look smaller.

They are farther away

from Earth.

# Kinds of Stars

Space is full of stars.

There are too many

stars to count.

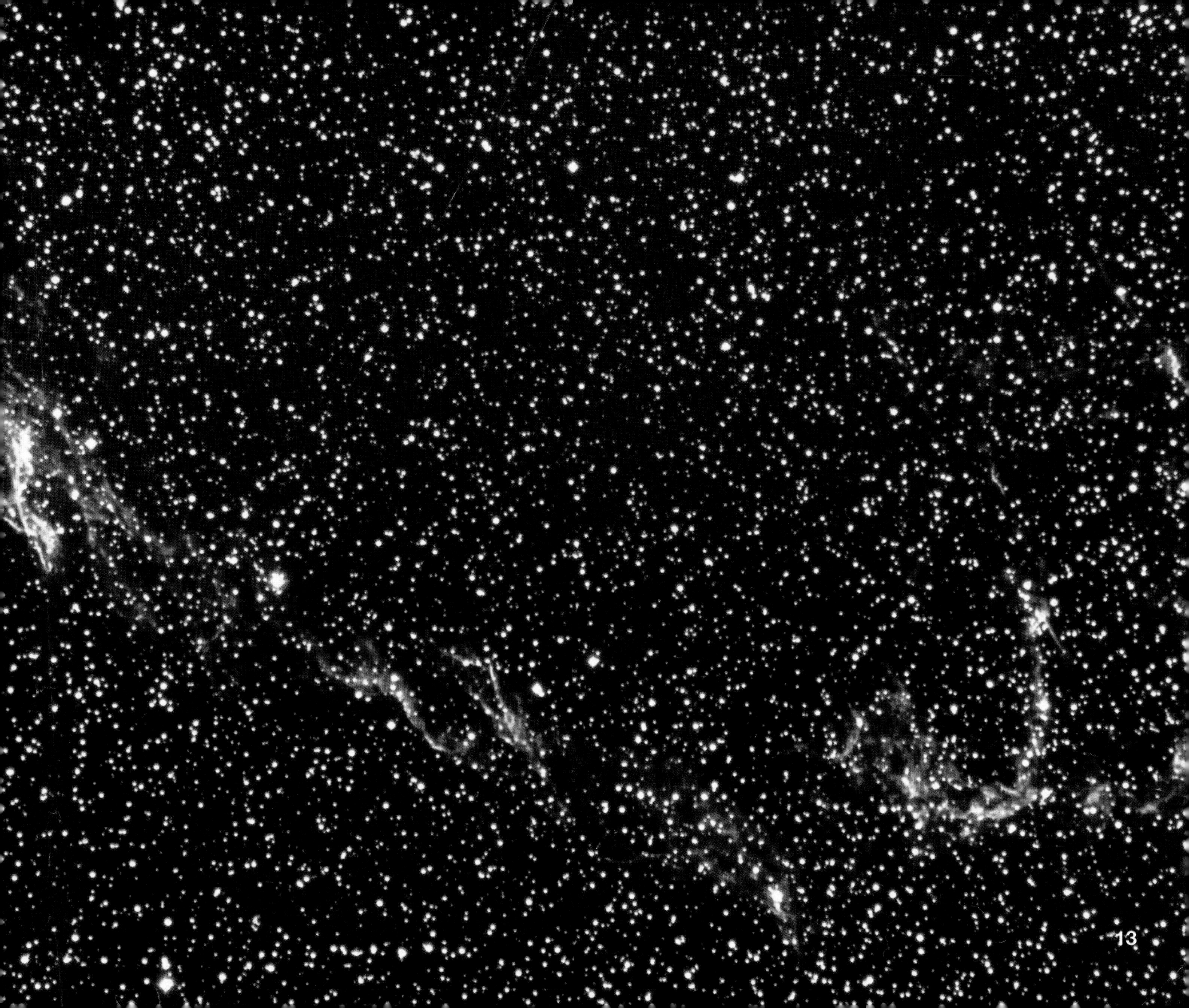

Some stars are yellow
like the Sun.
Other stars are white,
blue, red, or brown.

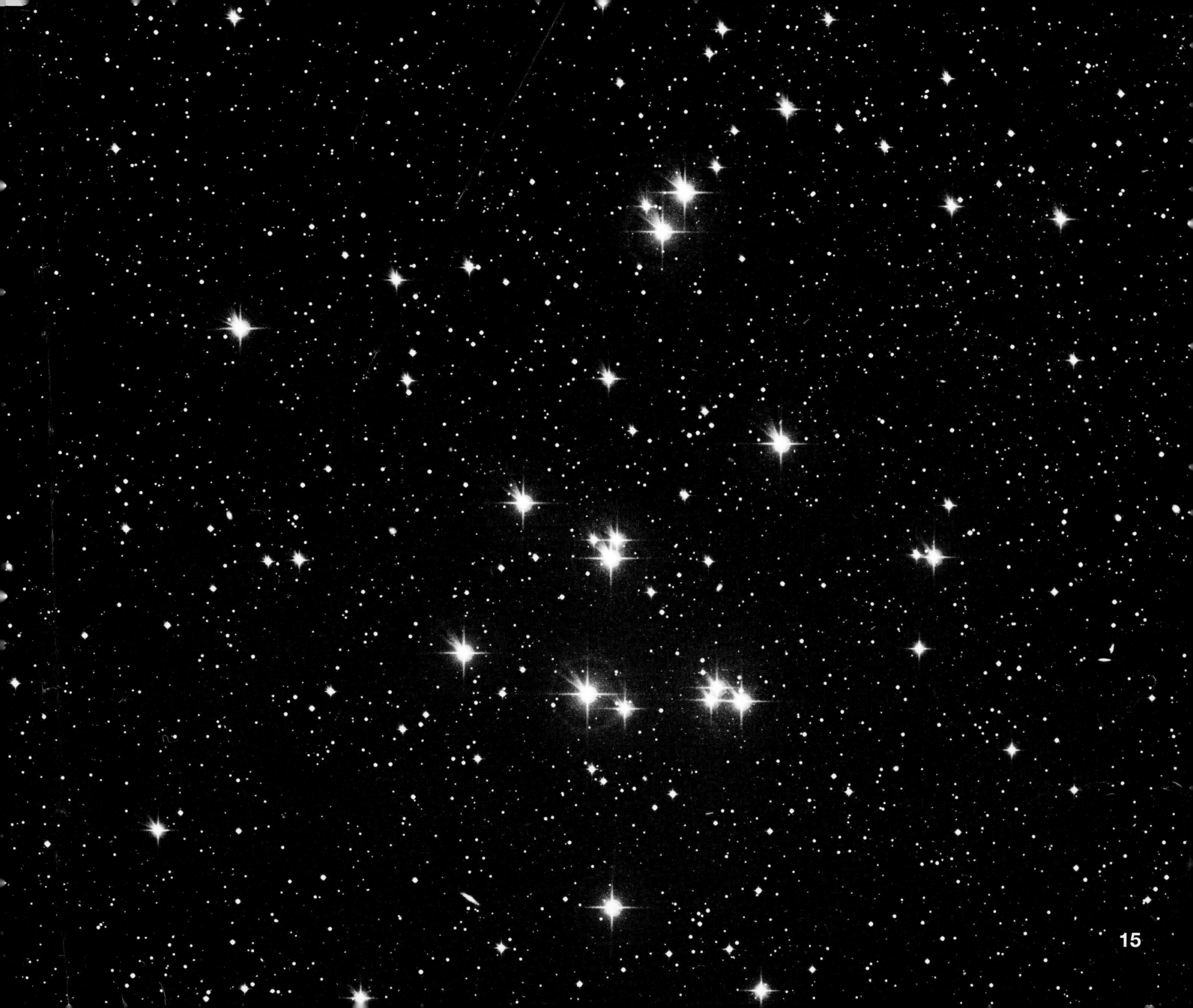

A star's color depends on
how hot it is.
Blue stars are the warmest.
Red stars are the coolest.

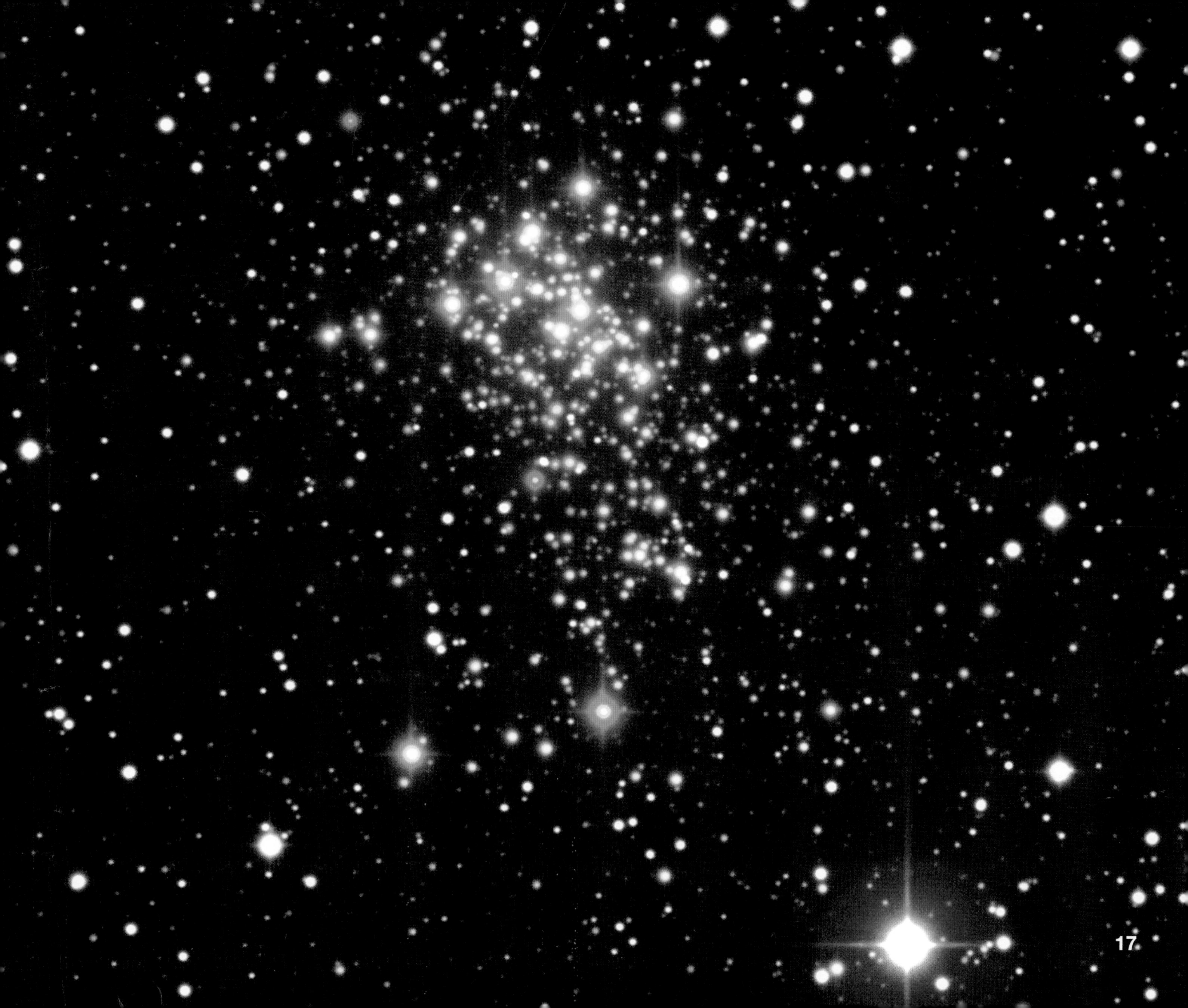

# Constellations

Groups of stars

form shapes in the sky.

The shapes

are called constellations.

19

Watch the stars twinkle!
How many stars do you
see in the night sky?

# Glossary

constellation—a group of stars that forms a shape

Earth—the planet we live on

gas—a substance that spreads to fill any space that holds it

space—the universe beyond Earth's atmosphere

star—a large ball of burning gases in space

Sun—the star that the planets move around; the Sun provides light and heat for the planets.

twinkle—to shine or sparkle; stars look like they twinkle because of movement in Earth's atmosphere.

# Read More

**Eckart, Edana.** *Watching the Stars.* Watching Nature. New York: Children's Press, 2004.

**Mitchell, Melanie.** *Stars.* First Step Nonfiction. Minneapolis: Lerner, 2004.

**Vogt, Gregory L.** *Constellations.* The Galaxy. Mankato, Minn.: Capstone Press, 2003.

# Internet Sites

FactHound offers a safe, fun way to find Internet sites related to this book. All of the sites on FactHound have been researched by our staff.

Here's how:

1. Visit *www.facthound.com*

2. Choose your grade level.

3. Type in the book ID **0736867465** for age-appropriate sites. You may also browse subjects by clicking on letters, or by clicking on pictures and words.

4. Click on the **Fetch It** button.

**FactHound will fetch the best sites for you!**

# Index

Word Count: 137
Grade: 1
Early-Intervention Level: 13